Books by Matt Christopher

Sports Stories

THE LUCKY BASEBALL BAT
BASEBALL PALS
BASKETBALL SPARKPLUG
TWO STRIKES ON JOHNNY
LITTLE LEFTY
TOUCHDOWN FOR TOMMY
LONG STRETCH AT FIRST BASE
BREAK FOR THE BASKET
TALL MAN IN THE PIVOT
CHALLENGE AT SECOND BASE
CRACKERJACK HALFBACK
BASEBALL FLYHAWK
SINK IT, RUSTY
CATCHER WITH A GLASS ARM
WINGMAN ON ICE
TOO HOT TO HANDLE
THE COUNTERFEIT TACKLE
THE RELUCTANT PITCHER
LONG SHOT FOR PAUL
MIRACLE AT THE PLATE
THE TEAM THAT COULDN'T
  LOSE
THE YEAR MOM WON THE
  PENNANT
THE BASKET COUNTS
HARD DRIVE TO SHORT
CATCH THAT PASS!

SHORTSTOP FROM TOKYO
LUCKY SEVEN
JOHNNY LONG LEGS
LOOK WHO'S PLAYING FIRST BASE
TOUGH TO TACKLE
THE KID WHO ONLY HIT HOMERS
FACE-OFF
MYSTERY COACH
ICE MAGIC
NO ARM IN LEFT FIELD
JINX GLOVE
FRONT COURT HEX
THE TEAM THAT STOPPED
  MOVING
GLUE FINGERS
THE PIGEON WITH THE TENNIS
  ELBOW
THE SUBMARINE PITCH
POWER PLAY
FOOTBALL FUGITIVE
THE DIAMOND CHAMPS

Animal Stories

DESPERATE SEARCH
STRANDED
EARTHQUAKE
DEVIL PONY

THE DIAMOND CHAMPS

MATT CHRISTOPHER

THE DIAMOND CHAMPS

Illustrated by Larry Johnson

BOSTON   **Little, Brown and Company**   TORONTO

FIRST EDITION

T 04/77

Library of Congress Cataloging in Publication Data

Christopher, Matthew F
  The diamond champs.

  SUMMARY: An aura of intrigue surrounds a baseball coach
obsessed with the idea of turning a bunch of handpicked
beginners into champions in one season.
  [1. Baseball—Fiction] I. Johnson, Larry.   II. Title.
PZ7.C458Di   [Fic]   76-56153
ISBN 0-316-13972-6

Published simultaneously in Canada
by Little, Brown & Company (Canada) Limited

PRINTED IN THE UNITED STATES OF AMERICA

To Vic and Bonnie

1962350

1

KIM! ON YOUR TOES!" yelled Coach Gorman E. Stag from home plate.

Heart pounding, Kim Rollins watched the coach toss the baseball up, then wallop it with his bat.

The ball shot up into the blue sky until it looked no larger than a pea, then started to descend.

"Stay with it, Kim!" cried Larry Wells, standing nearby with other outfielders of the Steelheads team.

Sure. It's easy for you to say, thought

1

Kim as he tried to judge where the ball was going to drop. *You've played before. I haven't. I'm as green as grass at this game. I shouldn't even be here!*

The ball was coming toward him. He raised his gloved hand, never taking his eyes off the fast-dropping sphere for a second. He had learned to do that much when he had missed the first three flies Coach Stag had knocked out to him.

Thunk! The ball dropped into the pocket of his glove and stuck there.

"Hey, man! You did it!" Larry exclaimed.

Someone applauded, and Kim blushed as he saw that it was Cathy Andrews, the only girl among the outfielders.

"Nice catch, Kim!" she said. "That was hit higher than the ones you missed, too!"

Kim took a deep breath, exhaled it, and winged the ball back in to home. Coach Stag praised him for the catch too, and proceeded to hit him another. Kim caught it, and caught the next, but dropped the fourth one.

"Okay, Kim!" yelled the coach. "You did all right! This one's for Cathy!"

He knocked one to her as high as he had for Kim. She got under it, caught it with no trouble, and threw it back in.

"Did Coach Stag call you up and ask you to play with the Steelheads, too?" Kim asked Cathy.

"Yes, he did. He called up everyone on the team."

"What about the infielders?" asked Kim curiously. "And the catcher? The pitcher? Where are they?"

"They're practicing tomorrow," Cathy answered.

"How do you know?" he asked.

She blew at a lock of hair that had fallen over her face. "Coach Stag asked Jo Franklin to play second base. She's a friend of mine and she told me."

Jo Franklin? He knew her, too. They

were in the same grade. A whiz kid in social studies. A wizard with a tennis racket. But a baseball player?

"Cathy, don't you get the feeling that something's really strange about Mr. Stag calling us all up and making a baseball team out of us?" Kim said. "Two girls, and me and the rest of the guys. I've never played baseball in my life, except pitch and catch. My bag is football and track."

"Then why are you here?"

"I don't *know*. I told him that I had never played before, but he said he didn't care. He'd have us practice every other day so that we'd learn the game as quickly as possible, and then enter us in the Bantam League. It sounded challenging. He wants us to win the championship."

"The championship?" echoed Larry. "He must be a dreamer! We'll end up at the bottom! That's where we'll end up."

"Bottom is right," admitted Kim glumly.

He began to wonder about the coach as

the short, barrel-chested man with dark sunglasses knocked out flies to Moe Harris and Sam Jacobs, the other outfielders. Who was he, anyway? None of the kids Kim had asked had ever heard of him before. And why was he so interested in organizing a team composed of both girls and boys? Although there was no ruling that a girl couldn't play on a boys' team in the Bantam League, most of the girls in town had their own baseball league.

Well, the only way to find out is to ask him, Kim said to himself.

After half an hour of catching fly balls, the players took batting practice. Coach Stag himself stood on the mound. He threw pitches that were easy to hit at first, then gradually he threw them faster.

The worst hitter of the lot was Kim. He remembered knocking out flies a few times while playing with friends, but that was before he had become interested in football and track. He couldn't remember ever picking up a bat once those activities had gotten into his blood, and could hardly believe that he was playing baseball now.

Man! he thought. *Coach Stag has certainly sweet-talked me into it!*

"Don't worry about it," the coach had said to him over the telephone when he had invited Kim to play on his new team. "You just come to the practices and do as I say. I'll mold you into a baseball player before the season's half over."

"But you *know* I've never been on a team before," Kim had told him. "I've hardly played at all in my whole life."

"I know, Kim," the coach had said. "But I still want you to play on my team. Why don't you stop worrying about it, okay? I'm the coach. Let me do the worrying. All I ask of you is to play. Can I have your word?"

Kim had taken a while to think about it. Finally he had agreed. "Okay, Mr. Stag. I'll play," he promised.

"Fine! I'm calling the team Steelheads,

Kim. It's a good, solid name to go with a good, solid team," Mr. Stag had said proudly.

Then he had named the practice dates, adding that he had already made arrangements for uniforms and all the other necessary equipment. He would even get Kim a glove if he didn't have one, he had said.

But Kim had remembered the old glove his father had sitting in the back porch closet. He had used it the few times he had played pitch and catch. It was still in good, usable condition.

So now here he was, being "molded" into a baseball player, as Coach Gorman E. Stag had promised.

Finally the coach called it quits, breathing tiredly himself after almost an hour of continuous practice. He was the only one wearing a baseball uniform, a plain white outfit with STEELHEADS printed across the front of the jersey. Kim had wondered when the players would be given theirs, but he wondered no longer as Coach Stag asked the outfielders to follow him to a blue car parked in the lot behind the third-base bleachers.

A man sitting behind the wheel got out as the group approached.

"Kids, meet Bernie Reese," said the coach. "He'll be my assistant."

While greetings were being exchanged, Kim saw a stack of white boxes piled on the back seat. He didn't need two guesses to know what was in them. The coach opened the door, took the boxes out one at a time, and handed them to the players.

"I've found out your sizes," he said, "so these uniforms should fit you perfectly."

Kim stared at him, but refrained from asking the coach any questions. He was too happy now anyway about getting a uniform — and a brand new one, at that.

Oohs and *aahs* bubbled from the players as they opened their boxes and dragged out their uniforms.

Coach Stag chuckled. "How about that?" he said. "Nice, aren't they?"

"They're beautiful!" Cathy exclaimed, her eyes wide and happy.

"They're far out, man," said Kim.

"Glad you like them," the coach replied. "Well, I've got to go. The next practice is the day after tomorrow. Same time, same place."

He opened the door on the passenger side of the car, and started to get in when Kim yelled to him, "Coach! Just a minute!"

"If you're wondering about our infield, Kim, they're practicing tomorrow!" called the coach as he got into the car. "See you the day after!"

"No, Coach!" Kim said. "It's something else!"

But the car had already backed up and was swinging around toward the road. Apparently the coach hadn't heard him.

2

PUFFBALL CLOUDS FLOATED across the sky the following afternoon as the Steelheads' infielders practiced. Jo Franklin, Cathy's friend, was alternating at second base with Roger Merts. She was wearing a baseball cap and shorts, and handling the grounders with the ease of an expert. As a matter of fact, Kim thought that she was even better than Roger, who acted somewhat nervous as Coach Stag's sizzling grounders came at him.

Eric Marsh, practicing at third base,

10

seemed uncomfortable in his position, too. He missed a few grounders before finally catching an easy hopper. Then his long, left-handed throw to first pulled A. J. Campbell off the base. But A. J., who seemed capable of handling his position, caught the ball easily, winged it back to Kim, and Kim threw it to Nick Forson, the Steelheads' catcher.

"That's crazy," said Larry Wells, sitting in the stands with Kim.

"What is?" Kim asked.

"A left-hander playing third base," replied Larry. "He should change positions with A. J. A right-hander can catch a ball and get the throw off quicker at third than a left-hander can. I don't get it."

Kim shook his head. "Neither do I. Man, Coach Stag sure has some weird ideas about organizing and coaching a team."

"Telling me?" said Larry. "I've never seen anything like it."

Kim smiled as a thought crossed his

mind. "Know what? It sure would be something if we won the championship!"

Larry laughed. "Win the championship? You're far out, man!"

Kim shrugged. Maybe he was, but the way Coach Stag was making the team practice could make winning the championship possible. Coach Stag was no ordinary coach. As a matter of fact, there was something very *extra-ordinary* about him. He was putting so much effort into training his players that you'd think he was getting paid for it.

Yet the method he was using to make a good, solid team was odd. He seemed to know and understand the game well, yet he had a few peculiar ideas. Whoever did hear of a left-hander playing third base? Could he possibly be seeing a potential in Eric's playing that position that other fans or players could not?

But what about me? Kim thought. *What potential could he see in me? I'm just a beginner. There must be other guys around he could have selected instead of me.*

But the team's roster had been formed, and the coach apparently wasn't going to change it.

There was a short, redheaded kid standing in front of the backstop wearing a glove, backing up the catcher on wild throws. Until now Kim hadn't paid any attention to him.

"What's Don Morgan doing here?" he asked finally, recognizing the boy, with whom he played football.

"I don't know." Larry cupped his hands and shouted. "Hey, Don! What are you doing? Chasing balls?"

Don turned, smiled, and shrugged. "I'm manager. When the league starts I'll be scorekeeper, too." Cupping his hands, he added in a lower voice, "It's for the birds!"

Kim laughed. "Good luck!" he said.

"What are you guys doing here?" Don inquired.

"We're outfielders," explained Kim. "We practiced yesterday, and we're practicing again tomorrow."

Don's eyes narrowed as they settled on Kim. "I thought you didn't play baseball."

"I'm playing now," replied Kim.

Don shook his head perplexedly as he turned away to chase after a ball that had bounced past the coach to the backstop.

It seemed, thought Kim, that he was learning something new about the Steelheads every time he saw another face. He was sure that Don had played on a team in the Bantam League that had finished in second or third place last year. Why would he want to play with the Steelheads this year, a brand new team that included at least one very inexperienced ballplayer?

"I can't believe that Don would take that job," he said. "He likes action, competition. You don't get any of that handling equipment or keeping score."

14

"It's Coach Stag," said Larry. "There's something about him and his strong will to have a winning team that really got to us."

"That must be it," agreed Kim. "He's got everybody really believing that."

"Right," said Larry.

After batting practice, Kim was amused to see Don picking up the bats and balls, and dumping them into a green canvas bag, while the infielders followed Coach Stag to the blue car behind the third-base bleachers to get their uniforms.

"Hurry up, Don!" Larry called to the manager. "Or you won't be getting a uniform!"

"That's what you think!" Don answered.

Kim and Larry left the stands, walked to the car, and watched the coach pass out the uniforms. The infielders' reaction was the same as the outfielders' had been yesterday, an assortment of happy *oohs* and *aahs*.

Kim noticed that Bernie Reese was again behind the wheel. *When is he going to start assisting Coach Stag?* Kim wondered. *Oh, well, obviously Coach Stag has his own peculiar way of doing things.*

He was handing out the uniforms so fast that Kim wondered whether Don Morgan would get there in time to receive his. It turned out that the coach had to wait about a minute for Don, who finally came on the run, carrying the equipment bag on his shoulders.

He ripped open his box as soon as the coach handed it to him, lifted out his sparkling white uniform, and held it up against him.

"It'll fit you," Kim assured him. "Don't worry about that."

The coach, lifting the equipment bag into the trunk of the car, shot him a sidelong glance and grinned. "Kim's right," he said. "The suits will fit you all

16

perfectly." Then he closed the trunk and got into the car. "Well, see you infielders and pitchers the day after tomorrow."

"Are we going to have a practice game before the league starts, Coach Stag?" Jo Franklin piped up.

"We certainly will," he answered. "But I want to make sure that we can make a decent showing first. Take care now!"

With that Mr. Reese started the car and they drove off.

"A decent showing?" Kim grimaced. "I could practice all summer and still wouldn't be able to make a decent showing!"

Larry laughed. "Maybe you'll surprise yourself," he said.

"I sure would!" said Kim. "Hey, Don," he went on, "if you think being manager is for the birds, why did you take the job?"

Don shrugged. "I don't know. I told the coach I would rather play, but he kept saying that a manager is almost as important as a player, and that a manager had to be really depended on, and he was sure he could depend on me."

"That's just what he said to me," said Brad Hamilton. "About depending on me, I mean."

"Me, too," said Jo. "But what's strange about that? You wouldn't want to play ball with *any* old coach, would you?"

"Right," agreed Doug Barton. "Coach Stag is number one in my book."

Kim looked at him. "Did you know him, Doug?"

"Not until now."

"Did any of you know him before he asked us to play on his team?" Kim inquired.

All said no.

"So what?" Doug scoffed. "Are we supposed to know all the grown-ups that live in Blue Hills? Don't make a big deal out of it."

He folded his uniform, stuck it back into

the box, and started to leave. "Anybody going my way?" he asked.

All but Larry and Kim took off with him.

"Come on," said Larry finally. "And forget about the coach, will you? So what if nobody knew him before? Like Doug said, it's no big deal."

3

DURING THE SECOND WEEK of
practice, the coach had the entire squad
working out together from two to three
hours a day. By Friday Kim saw an
improvement in himself that surprised
him, although he knew that a performance
in practice was often better than that in a
real game.

He had refrained from speaking to Larry
or anyone else on the Steelheads team
about Coach Stag, but in the meantime he

had learned that the parents of at least four team members didn't know Coach Stag either.

He tried not to let this knowledge bother him, telling himself that there was nothing odd about four parents in the whole town of Blue Hills not knowing Coach Stag. Blue Hills was a town of about fourteen thousand people. There must be a lot of people in that fourteen thousand who had never heard of him, just as there were a lot who had never heard of his own father.

The first practice game was played against the Red Arrows on Monday afternoon, just three weeks after the Steelheads team had been formed. The coach tacked the lineup on the dugout.

Eric Marsh	third base
Larry Wells	left field
Nick Forson	catcher
A. J. Campbell	first base
Brad Hamilton	shortstop

21

Kim Rollins	right field
Jo Franklin	second base
Cathy Andrews	center field
Doug Barton	pitcher

Utility infielders: Roger Merts and Jack Henderson
Utility outfielders: Moe Harris and Sam Jacobs
Utility pitcher: Russ Coletti

Both teams had batting and infield practices before the game got under way. It wouldn't have taken a baseball expert to determine which of the two was better. The Red Arrows, in their bright red uniforms, definitely outshone the Steelheads.

Doug Barton and the Red Arrows' Eddie Noles flipped for the choice of batting. Eddie won and chose to bat last. The umpire was Nick Forson's father, who agreed to do the job if everyone promised not to hit him if he made a bad call. The promise was unanimous.

Eric Marsh, leading off for the Steelheads, faced the Red Arrows' right-hander, Steve Wolzik, and was so nervous that he let four pitches go by without taking a swing. Two of them were strikes.

He swung on the next pitch and drilled it to short. Joe Fedderson, the shortstop, fielded the hop and rifled it to first for an out.

Larry Wells looked for the pitch he wanted, found it, swung at it, and flied out to center field. Nick hit a dribbler to third and almost beat it out. He might have, if he weren't so fat.

"You'd better run more and eat less," his father chided him. In the next instant Mr. Forson was yelling, "Okay, team! Hurry in! Hurry out!"

Mick Davis, leading off for the Red Arrows, hit Doug's first pitch to short. Brad caught the hop and heaved it to first. The throw was too wide and Mick ran to second on the overthrow.

Hank Stone flied out. Jim Kramer singled, scoring Mick, then sped to third on Fred Tuttle's left-center-field double.

"Let's settle down, Doug!" Kim yelled from right field. "Pitch it to 'im, kid!"

Duke Pierce walked to load the bases. Then Jim scored as Doug walked Ken Dooley, too.

Oh, man, thought Kim. *What a first inning this has turned out to be.*

Eddie Noles cracked a sharp grounder to short. Brad snared it, shot it to second. Second to first. A double play!

"Beautiful play, kids!" Coach Stag said cheerfully as the Steelheads came running in. "Okay, now. Let's get those two back."

A. J. Campbell struck out on three straight pitches.

"We can't do it that way, A. J.," mused the coach.

Brad pounded out a single, bringing up Kim.

I'll strike out. I know I will, he told himself.

"First of all, it's your mental attitude,"

his father had told him when Kim said he was going to play baseball with the Steelheads. "You have to build up a wall of confidence, telling yourself that you're going to do it and do it right. It's like anything else in this helter-skelter life of ours."

Kim tried to remember that as he swung at two pitches, missing them both. Then he let two wide ones go by, and swung at the next, a down-the-middle straight ball.

"Strike three!" yelled the ump.

I knew I'd strike out, he told himself bitterly.

Jo fouled a couple of pitches, then lashed out a single, advancing Brad to third. That was it as Cathy arced a fly to center field that was caught.

Joe Fedderson, leading off in the bottom of the second inning, lambasted Doug's first pitch for three bases, and the merry-go-round began, including a bases-loaded home run by Ken Dooley. The inning ended with the Red Arrows scoring six runs, bringing their total to eight.

"Eight to nothing," grumbled Kim as he sidled in between Larry and A. J. on the bench. "We're getting murdered!"

"Don't let it get you down," said Coach Stag from the corner of the dugout. "Most of you are still nervous. Don't worry. Playing this practice game is like getting the bugs out of a new car. By the time the league starts, you'll all be playing like last year's veterans." He paused, and chuckled. "Well, almost, anyway," he added.

It was the top of the third and Doug led off. *Crack!* He leaned into Steve's first pitch for a long shallow drive to left field for an easy double.

"On the go, gang!" Kim yelled, Doug's clout exciting him. "Blast it, Eric!"

Eric came through with a single, scoring Doug, and the ice was broken. But only A. J. managed to get another hit during that half of the inning. It was a single, not long enough to score Eric.

Again the Red Arrows enjoyed a hitting spree, including a double by Mick Davis with Steve Wolzik on base, and a triple by Jim Kramer, who scored on Kim's error in right field.

"Wow! Eleven to one!" Kim moaned as he trotted into the dugout.

"It should be only ten to one," Eric said, grinning.

"I know," Kim admitted, but avoided discussing the fly ball he had missed. Everybody, including himself, knew that he should have caught it.

"You're up, Kim!" called the coach. "Get your bat, fella!"

Kim had barely sat down. *That's right!* he thought, hopping out of the dugout. *That error must've shaken me up.*

He picked up his bat and hurried to the plate.

4

"STEEEERIKE!" BOOMED THE UMP.

Kim stepped out of the box, knowing that he would never see another pitch as good as that one was. He rubbed the sweat off his forehead and stepped back in.

"Ball!" The throw was wide.

"Ball two!" It was low.

He stepped out of the box again, rubbed his hands in the soft dirt, patted off the excess dust, and stepped back in. Nervously, he waited for Steve's next pitch.

It was in there. He swung. *Crack!* A long, high drive to deep center field!

It wasn't long enough. Duke Pierce, taking three steps backward, caught it handily.

Jo did no better, flying out to right field.

"Wait 'em out, Cathy," Coach Stag said to her as she started for the plate. "Let him pitch."

Cathy let five pitches go by for a three-two count, then cracked a double between left and center fields.

"Beautiful, Cathy!" yelled the Steelheads' fans.

Joe Fedderson missed Doug's sizzling grounder, and Cathy advanced to third. Then Hank Stone fumbled Eric's hot liner at third, and Cathy scored.

"See that?" said the coach. "They miss 'em, too."

Cathy can really hit, throw, and run, Kim thought. *So can Jo. But why did they agree to play with us? They could have made the girls' baseball league in town.*

The thought left his mind as he saw Larry lambaste a three bagger to deep left, driving in Doug and Eric. That was it as Nick, pounding a ground ball to deep short, again failed by a step to score a hit.

Eleven to four, the Red Arrows. *That's not so bad*, Kim thought. *We have two more bats coming. We can still show the Red Arrows we've got a pretty good ball team.*

The Red Arrows failed to score during their turn at bat, but so did the Steelheads in the top of the fifth. In the bottom of the inning, however, the Red Arrows picked up one run, and it looked as if the game would end soon as both Eric and Larry made outs in the sixth. But then the Steelheads saw a ray of hope as Nick walked, A. J. singled, and Brad walked, filling the bases.

"Keep us alive, Kim!" Coach Stag

shouted as Kim stepped to the plate, thinking nervously, *Why should I have to be the one to bat now?*

So far, his batting average was zero. He had struck out the first time up, and flied out the next two times. Steve Wolzik had nothing to worry about, even though he seemed to be a bundle of nerves on the mound.

"Ball one!" shouted the ump as Steve's first pitch to Kim missed the plate by inches.

"Ball two!" Inside.

"Ball three!" Again it was inside.

Third baseman Hank Stone trotted toward the mound, spoke a few seconds to Steve, then returned to his position.

Steve stretched, and pitched.

"Strike!" said the ump.

Then, "Strike two!"

Kim stepped out of the box, wiped his forehead, and heard the coach say, "Choke up on the bat, Kim!" He choked up on the bat and stepped into the box again. His palms were sweaty.

Steve whirled in the pitch. The ball shot in shoulder high, and Kim swung.

"Strike three!" yelled the ump as Kim's bat fanned the air.

It was over, the Red Arrows winning, 12 - 4.

"You guys and gals did fine," Coach Stag said happily as he called the team around him. "There is nothing to be ashamed of. I'm really proud of you, Kim." His eyes were almost invisible behind his dark sunglasses as he looked at Kim. "For hardly ever having played baseball at all before this year, your performance rates an A plus. Tell your dad that I'll make a baseball player out of you before the year's out!"

Kim smiled. *But I wonder why he'd think my father might be interested*, he thought.

"I want all of you here tomorrow evening, and every evening through Friday at six P.M. sharp," the coach went on. "Our first league game is a week from today, and I'm hoping that you'll make a good showing then, too. Okay! See you tomorrow!"

Not once during the week had anyone failed to show up at practice. Coach Stag was proud of the team's dedication, and promised that if the players kept up that spirit they might just finish the season as champions.

There was something else that he wanted the players to learn, and that was a simple series of signs. They were "wait out the pitch," "hit away," "bunt," and "steal."

By six o'clock Monday, when the Steelheads played the Herons in their first league game, the players were as familiar with the signs as they were with their own names.

The Herons had first bats, and did nothing. Russ Coletti, who was pitching

33

this game, served up left-handed pitches that set them down one, two, three.

Eric, leading off for the Steelheads in the bottom of the first, drew a walk, then raced to second on Brad's sacrifice bunt. He perished there as A. J. struck out, and Larry flied out to center.

Two errors and a hit put the Herons on the scoreboard for two runs in the top of the second. It wasn't till the bottom of the third that the Steelheads came alive again, spurred by Eric's walk, Brad's double, Larry's triple, and Cathy's single.

In the bottom of the fourth Jo led off with a double, a blast between left and center fields, and scored on Russ's Texas Leaguer over short. The score was 4 - 2, in the Steelheads' favor, as the game went into the fifth inning.

"I can't believe it!" A. J. exclaimed as he ran out to the field with Kim. "We're ahead, man!"

"And by two runs!" Kim smiled, even though he had done nothing in the batting department so far to help the Steelheads.

Then the dam collapsed. The Herons got onto Russ's pitches and hit him for four runs, one of which was a homer by Dick Algren, the Herons' eighth batter in their lineup.

"Man, I can't believe it, Kim!" cried A. J., as he ran off the field with Kim. "Four runs! Just like that!"

"Well, it isn't over yet," said Kim, who had more confidence now in the Steelheads than he had ever dreamed he would. "We were ahead before, we can get ahead again."

Cathy, leading off, pulled a walk. Then Kim, swinging and missing the first two pitches, connected with the third one. *Boom!* Instantly he knew that he had just hit the most solid drive in his brief baseball career. Dropping the bat and starting for first, he watched the ball sail deep out to left field, then disappear over the fence. A home run!

He circled the bases, crossed the plate, and received an overwhelming ovation from the fans and his teammates.

"Man!" cried A. J. as he shook Kim's hand. "I can't believe it! You really busted that one, man!"

Kim grinned. "I can't believe it either," he admitted, half in a daze.

The two runs, all that the Steelheads earned that half inning, had tied up the score.

Then the Herons came back again, scoring three runs to boost their tally to nine.

"This is our last chance," said Coach Stag, clapping his hands to stimulate his charges. "Let's go, gang! Let's go get 'em!"

Eric flied out to left field, and Brad grounded out to short. Things didn't look good.

Then A. J. connected with a sharp single

through the hole at short. Larry, with a triple in the third inning, connected with a triple again! And Cathy, already with a single and a walk to her credit, banged out another single, scoring Larry!

"One more run will tie it up!" yelled the coach enthusiastically, and every member of the team stood up, feeling that same enthusiasm, that same excitement.

"Another homer, Kim!" Eric shouted, as Kim stepped into the batter's box. "You can do it, kid!"

Kim hit the ball solidly, but it was a direct shot to the left fielder.

He was out, and the game went to the Herons, 9 - 8.

5

I JUST REMEMBERED THAT I won't be able to make practice tomorrow," Eric said to Kim as they started to leave the ball field together.

"So what?" said Kim. "Coach Stag isn't going to boot you off the team just because you can't make practice."

"Yes, but I hate not to show up without telling him," Eric replied disappointedly.

"Well —" Kim glanced over his shoulder. "He's gone now. So call him up. He'd appreciate it."

"I think I will," agreed Eric.

It was almost two hours later when Kim received a phone call from Eric.

"Know what? I don't think Coach Stag lives in Blue Hills," said Eric.

Kim frowned. "How do you know that?"

"His name isn't in the phone book. There is no *Stag* in there."

"Well, how about that?" said Kim. He paused. "Eric, have you ever asked your parents if they know Coach Stag?"

"Yes, I have, and they don't," he said.

"Okay. Well, don't worry about not letting him know that you can't make practice tomorrow. I'll tell him you tried to call him but couldn't find his name in the book."

"Okay, Kim. Thanks."

Kim hung up, wondering: *If Coach Stag doesn't live in Blue Hills, where does he live? The nearest village is Croydon, which is at least ten miles away. He could live in the country, but even so his name would be listed in the phone directory if he had a phone.*

Maybe he lives in one of the half-dozen other towns listed in the directory, Kim thought. *If not, he just doesn't have a phone, that's all.*

He picked up the directory and checked each town thoroughly for *Stag*. There were two listed in the town of Hayden, *Stag, Henry*, and *Stag, Kermit*, the only Stags in the book.

Maybe they're relatives, he thought. *Maybe they know where Gorman E. Stag lives.*

Vaguely worried, Kim put the directory away and walked into the living room, hoping he could forget about Coach Stag. He didn't know why he should let the coach bother him so, anyway. *No one else on the team seems concerned about him, so why should I be?* Kim thought.

But it was impossible to erase the coach

from his mind. Maybe it was because of his natural bent to be suspicious. His favorite books were detective stories and mysteries, science fiction running a close second. He had often daydreamed about working in a crime laboratory when he grew up. Dusting for fingerprints and searching for clues seemed like an exciting career, he figured. At the same time he'd help bring criminals to justice.

Of course Coach Stag is no criminal, Kim told himself. But *why* he picked up a brand new team, *why* he included an inexperienced player like Kim on it, and *why* he was anxious to have a good winning ball team were questions that needed answers. And only Coach Stag knew them.

Someday I'm going to get up enough nerve to ask him, Kim promised himself.

At practice the next afternoon he told the coach about Eric. "He tried to phone you," said Kim, "but he couldn't find your name in the phone book."

"I don't have a phone," the coach admitted. "Eric is all right, I hope?"

"Yes. He just couldn't come today, that's all. He didn't tell me why."

"Okay." The coach smiled. "Thanks for telling me, Kim." He turned to Don Morgan. "Get the bats and balls out of the bag, Don. Hurry it up. We're a little late."

As Don began to loosen the string of the equipment bag, Kim considered asking the coach the questions that were constantly gnawing at his mind. *Why did you pick up a team, Coach? Why did you ask me to be on it? And why are you so anxious to have a good winning ball team?* But at the last minute he found his tongue tied. While he fought a mental battle to regain his courage, the coach's loud voice shattered his thoughts.

"Okay, everybody except Brad, A. J. and

Larry, out on the field!" he ordered. "Doug, throw 'em in!"

Batting practice was starting. After the players batted around twice, the coach knocked out flies to the outfielders while Bernie Reese hit grounders to the infielders.

The practice, a very thorough one, lasted an hour and a half. When it was over the coach informed the tired players that practice tomorrow would be at Lansdale Field, the other baseball park where the games were being played.

"Can you give Eric that message, Kim?" asked the coach as he started to carry the equipment bag to his car.

"Yes," said Kim.

"Fine. See you all tomorrow. Same time."

Mr. Reese unlocked the trunk of the car and the coach laid the bag into it. Then they entered the car and drove away.

"Brad, did you ever practice so much last year when you played baseball?" Kim asked wonderingly, so tired he wanted to lie down.

"Never."

"Me, either," said A. J. "The way Coach Stag is working us out you'd think that he was *serious* about us winning the championship!"

Practice the next day lasted only an hour and fifteen minutes. The whole squad was there except Coach Stag. There was no explanation of his absence, but the practice went along very well. Mr. Reese seemed to understand the game as well as Coach Stag.

If anybody knows where the coach lives, Mr. Reese should, thought Kim.

"Mr. Reese, where does Coach Stag live?" he asked. "I've looked for his name in the phone book, but I can't find it."

Mr. Reese, lifting the filled equipment bag to his shoulder, glanced at Kim.

"On Beaver Street," he answered. "Six seventeen Beaver. Why?"

Kim shrugged. "I just wanted to know."

6

WHEN THE STEELHEADS tangled
with the Magpies, both teams were hitting
well as the game went into the top of the
fourth inning. The Steelheads led, 4 - 3.
Doug was pitching, and the Magpies were
at bat.

Crack! A Magpie hit a shot over second
base for a clean single. Another single and a
walk loaded the bases. And Kim, in right
field, couldn't believe how a situation
could become so grim so quickly.

Doug proceeded to take his time now,

obviously not happy by the sudden turn of events. He stretched, and threw. *Crack!* The ball, an outside pitch to the right-handed batter, sailed out to deep right. Kim backed up, his heart rising to his throat as he saw how high the ball had climbed into the blue sky. He waited for it to drop. It was like a white pea, gradually growing larger as it kept coming down. Holding his glove in readiness for it, Kim held his breath.

The ball hit the heel of his glove, dropped to the ground, and bounced away. Kim bolted after it, scooped up the ball, and heaved it to first base. He could see that a runner had crossed the plate, and that a second runner was on the way home.

A. J., catching Kim's throw, turned and whipped the ball home. The throw was high. The runner slid in to the plate and scored.

Five to four, Magpies. Runners were still on second and third.

Why wasn't that ball hit to left field, or center field? Kim thought despairingly. *Why did it have to be hit to me?*

A double scored two more runs before Doug fanned two batters. The third out came on a pop fly to Eric. Seven to four.

"I don't know why you ever asked me to play, Coach," said Kim cheerlessly as he came in and sat down on the bench. "I should've caught that ball in my hip pocket."

"If you did, you'd have major league scouts looking you over." The coach smiled. "Listen, Kim, playing baseball is like a lot of things in life, except that it has something extra to it. Fun. Otherwise, it's just as competitive as anything else you'll ever come up against the rest of your life. I know that it's been very new to you, and that's good. You've learned the game, and the rules. You've met with some successes, and some failures. Kim, it wasn't all an easy thing for Hank Aaron to have broken Babe Ruth's home-run record, you know. He had gotten out many times before that had happened. It's the same with football or basketball players, the same with doctors, lawyers, teachers, cops — everyone who tries to make something of himself in this big, competitive world of ours knows something about failure."

He slapped Kim on the knee and stood up. "Just keep plugging, Kim. No one is going to bawl you out for missing a fly as long as you do your best in trying to catch it. Okay?"

Kim, feeling much better, nodded. "Okay."

The Steelheads went hitless as Nick grounded out to short, and Jo and Doug flied out to the outfield.

The Magpies got a man on in the top of the fifth, but failed to knock him in. Eric, leading off for the Steelheads, cracked a single. But he too failed to score as the

Magpies' defense gobbled up the balls hit out to them.

In the top of the sixth the Magpies' leadoff batter walked, then scored on an over-the-left-field-fence home run — 9 - 4, Magpies.

Cathy, first up for the Steelheads in the bottom of the sixth, doubled to get them rolling for their last chance to win, then scored on Kim's Texas Leaguer hit over short. But that was it. Neither Nick nor Jo was able to connect safely, and the game went to the Magpies, 9 - 5.

"I heard that speech Coach Stag gave you in the dugout," Doug said to Kim as they headed for the gate. "What do you think of him now?"

"I think he's all right," replied Kim. "I have, ever since he organized the team. I've just wondered why he's done it, that's all."

"Because he wants to win the championship, that's why," said Doug.

"Don't you think it's strange that he picked up a team like us to win it?"

"Maybe most kids were already signed up to play with other teams," replied Doug. "I wasn't when he called me."

"Well, no one was. But I still think it's real strange," commented Kim.

They walked through the gate and headed up the street.

"Did you ever notice the sound of his voice?" asked Cathy suddenly.

Kim looked at her. "Yes. Especially when he was talking to me today. It's kind of raspy. Is that what you mean?"

"Yeah!" said Nick, his eyes widening. "I've noticed it, too! It sounds as if he's trying to change it from what it *really* sounds like!"

"How do you know?" said Doug. "We've only known him since baseball season started. Maybe he's always talked like that."

"Come to think of it, I've noticed that,

too," said Jo. "I've always thought it was natural, though. But I've also noticed something else that looks strange about him."

Kim frowned. "What, Jo?"

"His chest," she replied. "It's almost rounded, as if he's got it built up. And ever since we've seen him he's always worn that same baseball jersey. Never anything else, like a sweatshirt, for example."

Kim nodded. "That's right," he said. "Maybe he's someone we know. Maybe, for reasons of his own, he's disguised himself to hide his real identity."

"Could he be a criminal?" Jo asked breathlessly.

All eyes swung toward her.

"What about that speech he gave you?" Doug said to Kim. "Do you really think a criminal would bother to talk to you like that? Do you really think a criminal would take the time to knock out flies and grounders, and teach us how to play better baseball? If you do, you're out of your mind!"

Striking a fist into the pocket of his glove, he took off on a run, and soon was far ahead of the rest of the Steelheads.

7

THE STEELHEADS PLAYED two games the next week, beating the Fire Fighters 7 - 4, and losing to the Red Arrows, 10 - 9.

The fifty percent average didn't satisfy the coach, however. "We've got to play better ball, kids," he insisted. "We've just got to. Okay?"

Kim paid special attention now to the coach's raspy voice. Was it natural, or was the coach trying to disguise his real voice?

Or, as Jo had suggested, was he really a criminal of some sort?

In spite of Doug's scoffing at Jim and Jo for that wild suggestion, Kim didn't think that the idea was too farfetched. A. J. and Brad thought that they were nuts too for even thinking it, but Kim wouldn't change his mind. He refused to be convinced that the coach *was* or *was not* an outlaw until he got proof who the coach really was.

But how was he going to do that?

I'll go to 617 Beaver Street, thought Kim. *That's how. I'll pay him a visit. I'll tell him that I was walking by and just wanted to say hello.*

The more he thought about it the more nervous he became. Suppose the coach really was a bad guy? What then? What would he say? What would he do?

Kim considered asking Eric to go with him. Two would be better than one, he thought. Moreover, a second person could provide proof of whatever Kim found out.

He mulled over the idea for an hour, then telephoned Eric and explained his plan. The wire was silent for a moment, and Kim wondered if Eric was reluctant to go with him.

"I don't know, Kim," Eric answered finally. "Do you think that's a good idea?"

"How else can we find out who the coach really is?" said Kim.

"Ask him."

"*Ask* him?" echoed Kim. "*Me* ask him?"

"Well, you're the one who wonders more about who the coach is than anyone else on the team," replied Eric. "Yes, I think you should be the one to ask him."

"Then you don't want to go with me to his home?"

"Why don't you ask him at Monday's practice?"

"Not with all the kids around, I won't," said Kim.

"Okay. Will you ask him if I go with you?"

Kim hesitated. "No," he said honestly. "Look, Eric, why don't we just go to his home? Can't we just tell by the way he lives whether he's a crook?"

"It sounds crazy," Eric said.

"Then you don't want to go?"

"I told you, Kim. It sounds crazy. Just think about it. Doesn't it sound crazy?"

"I've already thought about it," said Kim. "Okay. See you at practice."

At practice on Monday, neither Kim nor Eric said anything more about visiting the coach at his home. Nothing was said on Tuesday either, although there were suspicious glances exchanged between Eric, Jo, Doug, and Kim. Kim hoped that the coach didn't become suspicious himself about the strange behavior of the kids. If he did, he kept it to himself. Which was strange, if you thought of it, Kim mused. Wouldn't it be natural for the coach to question them if he saw that they were behaving unnaturally?

It seemed, though, that all the coach was really interested in was training the team to win ball games.

"We're playing the Blue Jays tomorrow," he said after Tuesday's practice. "Let's make up our minds that we'll beat them, okay? It's that mental attitude that counts. Always that mental attitude."

And always that first and foremost thought, Kim reflected. *To win the championship*.

There was a change in the lineup for the Blue Jays game.

Roger Merts	third base
Larry Wells	left field
Nick Forson	catcher
A. J. Campbell	first base
Jack Henderson	shortshop
Sam Jacobs	right field
Jo Franklin	second base
Moe Harris	center field
Doug Barton	pitcher

So I'm not playing today, thought Kim. *He's giving us turns, which is okay with me.*

It made more sense to play Roger at third than Eric, anyway, Kim reflected as he watched the right-hander throwing the ball to first in the pregame practice. After all this time, Eric was still awkward in throwing the ball left-handed to first base after catching a grounder. It would certainly seem obvious to the coach, but do you think he'd make a change? No. It seemed that he had a special reason for playing Eric there.

The Steelheads had first bats, and Roger started off the game with a hot grounder through short. Larry bunted him to second. And Nick, after fouling two pitches to the backstop, cracked a two bagger that scored Roger. Anyone else except heavy-footed Nick might have stretched the hit into a triple.

61

A. J. went down swinging, and Jack popped out to second — 1 - 0, Steelheads.

The Blue Jays threatened to score when they got two men on base with two hits, but strong defensive plays after that kept the runners from scoring.

It wasn't until the fourth inning that the Steelheads' bats began pounding out hits again. A. J. got a triple with two on, and then scored on Jack's smashing single over short. Jo kept up the rally with a double, and then scored on Moe's streaking hit over the third-base bag. Five runs crossed the plate before the Blue Jays managed to stop them — 6 - 0, Steelheads.

The kids were happy, but the coach was even happier.

"With that lead we should coast," he said, a tone of merriment in his raspy voice. "But we won't. We're not going to take a single chance of losing."

The team nodded as a unit. Kim met Doug's eyes. *Well, do you still think he's some sort of crook?* they seemed to ask.

I'm still not sure, Kim wanted to reply.

The Blue Jays picked up a run in the bottom of the fifth and two in the bottom of the sixth. But the three runs weren't enough. The Steelheads took the game, 6 - 3.

"Nice playing, gang!" Coach Stag praised the team. "Let's keep it up! We'll win the championship if you play as you did today. I know we will."

"Is there practice tomorrow, Coach?" Jo asked.

"Yes. But not on Monday," replied the coach. "We've got two games next week. I'm hoping that we won't have to practice in between games anymore."

Jo's eyes shone. "I wouldn't care," she said. "I love it!"

"So do I," admitted Nick.

From the pleased looks on the faces of the other players, Kim was sure that none of them minded the practices either, even though the practices were usually tougher than the games.

"It will depend, though," said the coach. "If we start losing, we will practice. So let's keep winning. Okay, see you tomorrow."

Mr. Rollins walked home with Kim and Eric. This was the second game he had attended, and he seemed impressed by the Steelheads' showing.

"You kids played real well," he said. "I'm surprised, though, that Coach Stag didn't have you all play."

"He's got a system of his own, Dad," explained Kim. "His lineup is different for each game, but there are no substitutions. Anyone who doesn't play in one game will play in the next."

His father shrugged. "That is different, all right." Then he chuckled, and added, "Watching you kids play makes me realize how time flies. I only know a few of the kids on your team, but I used to play with their fathers. Know what that means? I'm getting old, man!"

"What position did you play, Mr. Rollins?" Eric asked.

"Right field."

"The same as me," said Kim.

"Hey, that's a coincidence," said Eric, wide-eyed with surprise. "I play third, and my dad used to play third."

Kim looked at him. "Is your father left-handed like you are?"

"No."

"Lars?" Mr. Rollins chuckled. "He was definitely right-handed, and one of the best third basemen in northern New York. I've never seen anyone who fielded bunts as he did, nor who could throw as hard. If he were able to hit as well as field, he would've gone up to the big leagues."

Eric grinned. "My mother used to say the same thing, Mr. Rollins," he said proudly.

8

THE STEELHEADS WON THE next two games, beating the Herons and the Magpies for a record of four wins against three losses.

"We're getting there," said Coach Stag. "Slowly but surely we're getting there."

He seemed extremely pleased, yet Kim noticed that his facial expression hardly changed. *I wish I could see his eyes*, Kim thought. But they were shielded, as always, behind the dark sunglasses.

The next game was on Wednesday

66

against the Red Arrows. It was the only game the Steelheads had scheduled for that week. Doug was pitching and not doing as well as he had in previous games, yielding five hits and four runs in the first two innings.

The Steelheads, batting in the top of the third, again went through the half inning without a run in spite of Doug's two-base hit. But they held the Red Arrows scoreless in the bottom half of the inning. Did that mean anything? Were the Steelheads showing some improvement? *I sure hope so*, thought Kim, as Larry Wells stepped to the plate to start off the top of the fourth inning.

Steve Wolzik, pitching for the Red Arrows, tried to bait Larry with wide and inside pitches, but Larry refused to bite. After a three-two count, Larry took another ball and walked.

"Wait 'em out, Cathy," advised the coach, as Cathy Andrews strode to the plate, snuggling the helmet down over her locks.

She took two strikes, then checked her swing from a pitch that turned out to be a ball. Steve missed the strike zone with another. Then Cathy socked a knee-high pitch directly to Mick Davis, who was covering second base. Mick flipped the ball to second to nab Larry. Joe Fedderson, the Red Arrows' sparkling shortstop, zipped the ball to first for a quick double play.

Kim, starting for the plate, saw the coach swing around and kick angrily at the sod. But he quickly turned back, apparently composed again, and began clapping his hands. "Okay, Kim!" he yelled. "It's never too late! Get your hit!"

Kim did, smashing a single over second base. Nick followed suit, driving a single through short that advanced Kim to third. Kim slid into the bag on the throw in from center, safe by a yard.

"Drive 'em in, Jo!" yelled Moe Harris, the third-base coach.

Crack! It was another single, a high hopping grounder through second. Mick, making a dive for it, almost caught it. The ball bounced out to left center field and Kim ran in to score. Nick started for third, but Moe held him back.

Doug, up next, walked, loading the bases.

Excitement bubbled among the players on the Steelheads' bench. The top of the batting order was up: Eric, Brad, and A. J. They were the best hitters on the club. But there were two outs. Eric, even though he hadn't hit safely yet, had been meeting the ball. This could be his right moment.

It was! He laid into Steve's first pitch and lambasted it for a double between left and center fields! Nick and Jo scored.

"Keep it up, Brad!" yelled Coach Stag. "Just meet the ball!"

Brad met the ball, but it was a line drive directly at Joe Fedderson. Three outs.

"That's all right!" cried Coach Stag happily. "We've picked up three runs! We'll pick up more!"

Again the Red Arrows failed to score, not even getting a hit as Doug mowed down the batters, one . . . two . . . three.

A. J., leading off in the top of the fifth, pulled a walk, and Kim's heart began to pound. *Is this going to be a repetition of the fourth inning?* he thought excitedly.

Larry powdered a fly to left field. It was caught.

"Darn!" said Kim under his breath.

Cathy took a ball, a strike, then belted a low pitch through the hole between first and second bases. Like a frightened rabbit, A. J. bolted to second, then to third.

"Keep up the rally, Kim!" Moe yelled from his third-base coaching box.

Kim took two called strikes, then struck

out. He returned to the dugout, his heart sick.

"Chin up, Kim," said the coach. "We're still in there."

Nick dodged a close pitch, falling down to get out of its way. Glaring at the pitcher, he got up and stood with his bat held high, waving it like a club.

"He didn't like that close pitch," said Kim. "If Steve puts one in there, it's good-bye."

Steve put one in there. And it was good-bye. The long, solid drive carried far over the left field fence for a home run, and Nick trotted around the bases with an ear-to-ear grin on his face.

The whole team met him at the plate and shook his hand.

"What power, man!" Kim smiled at him.

Jo flied out to center to end the half inning — 6 - 4, Steelheads.

Mick Davis, leading off for the Red

Arrows in the bottom of the fifth, latched onto a high pitch to deep right. The ball bounced in front of Kim, slipped through his legs, and rolled to the fence.

"Rats!" he fumed, spinning on his heels and sprinting after the ball. By the time he whipped it to the infield, Mick was safe on third.

Doug struck out Hank Stone, then walked Jim Kramer, who had already accumulated two safe hits. Fred singled, scoring Mick, putting the Red Arrows just one run behind.

Then Duke Pierce popped out to short and Ken Dooley fanned, bringing the threatening half inning to an end — 6 - 5, Steelheads.

"Our last time up," reminded Coach Stag. "Let's chalk up a few more runs, shall we?"

Doug waited out Steve's pitches, finally flying out to center field.

Again the top of the batting order was up.

"Don't get too anxious now, Eric," cautioned the coach calmly as the left-handed third baseman and hitter stepped to the plate. "Wait for the one you like."

Eric nonetheless seemed nervous as he waved the bat back and forth, his legs spread wide, his attention riveted on the pitcher. He took two called strikes, fouled a pitch — and then blasted a line drive over short for a clean single!

The whole team shouted their approval, then shouted even louder as Brad stepped to the plate and lambasted a fence-hitting triple, scoring Eric.

A. J., with just a walk to his credit so far, cracked a streaking single through the mound. Steve made a vain effort to catch it, but the hit was clean, and another run scored.

Larry lifted a long fly to left that Jim Kramer pocketed in his glove. Two outs.

But that didn't seem to dim Cathy's hopes as she swung at a waist-high pitch and rocketed it for a long double to right center, scoring A. J.

Kim, hoping he could continue the hitting spree, managed to make first all right, but it was due to an error by shortstop Joe Fedderson. Cathy advanced to third on the play, but perished there as Nick flied out to left.

Trailing 9 - 5, the Red Arrows made a bold attempt to catch up as Eddie Noles cracked Doug's first pitch for a double. Joe flied out to left, but Larry's strong arm kept Eddie from advancing.

Steve, considered to be one of the league's best hitting pitchers, proved his worth as he laced an outside corner pitch for a single, scoring Eddie.

The Red Arrows were closing the gap, 9 - 6. And the top of their batting order was up.

9

MICK DAVIS, THE RED ARROWS'
leadoff batter, stood at the plate and
watched three pitches zip by him without
taking the bat off his shoulder. All three
pitches were balls.

Nick called time and ran out to the
mound. He talked with Doug a bit, then
returned to his position behind the plate.

Doug removed his cap, brushed back his
hair, pulled his cap back on, and stepped
on the rubber. He stretched, checked the

runner on first, then breezed in the pitch.

"Strike!" cried the ump.

"Nice pitch, Doug!" Nick shouted.

Doug pitched again. "Strike two!"

Doug put the next one in there too, and Mick swung. *Crack!* It was a blazing shot to right field, curving toward the foul line!

Kim bolted after it. At the last instant he stretched out his gloved hand to catch it, but the ball hit the tip of his glove and bounced to the outfield. Kim chased after it, realizing that it was the second time he had missed a ball in this game. He picked it up near the fence, turned, and heaved it in. Steve was running in to score, and Mick was sprinting to third.

Slapping his fist disgustedly into the pocket of his glove, Kim told himself again that he had no business being here. He was no outfielder. He wasn't even a baseball player. Coach Stag had been trying to mold him into one, and was failing at it. *He could never mold me into a baseball player*, Kim reflected. *Never. So missing that fly wasn't really my fault*.

He pushed his thoughts aside as Hank Stone stepped to the plate. Hank waited out Doug's pitches too, then slammed a hot liner toward short. The ball started to zoom over Brad's head, and Brad leaped, his gloved hand held high. The ball smacked into its pocket for an out.

Quickly he whipped the ball to third as Mick, about five steps off the base, tried to get back.

Eric caught the ball in time, and Mick was out. Three outs. The ball game was over, and the Steelheads took it, 9 - 7.

Relieved, Kim ran in and joined in congratulating Brad for the play that saved the game for the Steelheads.

And for Coach Stag.

"Great catch, Brad," he praised. "That's another one in the bag."

Kim looked at him, and saw the coach's intense gaze. "You made a real gallant effort on that hit, Kim," said the coach. "Almost had it, too. Good hustling."

Kim frowned. "It was an error, wasn't it?"

"Error nothing. It was a genuine hit. And we won despite it."

Kim felt a little better, but what really began to lie heavily on his mind was the coach's attitude about winning. Nothing else seemed to be more important to Coach Stag, as if he were trying to get his name, and the names of the Steelheads, in the record books.

Why was he so fanatic about winning, anyway? It was the umpteenth time that the question stood so uppermost in Kim's mind.

Late the next afternoon he was making a peanut butter sandwich when Mr. Rollins called to him from the living room. Kim went out there, pressing the two slices of bread tightly together.

"Yes, Dad?" he said as he saw his father sitting in an armchair, reading the *Blue Hills Citizen*.

"I was reading about the game," he said, turning to Kim. "I notice by the names of the kids who play on the Steelheads team that some of them don't live in the neighborhood. Isn't there a ruling that says they should?"

"I don't know. But I guess not, Dad. Just like a few of the other teams, some of our team live in other parts of Blue Hills."

"I see that," replied his father. "The Forsons and the Wellses live on the north side. I used to play ball with their fathers. And this A. J. Campbell. He's probably Tony Campbell's son."

Kim shrugged. "Could be, Dad." Then he frowned. "Did you play baseball with his father, too?"

"I sure did. He was tall, left-handed, and played first base."

Kim's eyebrows knitted. "So does A. J."

"I see that," said his father. "And he's right-handed."

He read further and chuckled. "Well, how about that?" he said. "Rollins, right field; Forson, catcher; Franklin, second base; Barton, pitcher."

"Do you recognize those other names, Dad?" Kim inquired curiously.

"I sure do," answered Mr. Rollins. "Dominic Forson was our catcher, Andy Franklin our second baseman and Junk Barton one of our pitchers. We called him Junk because of the junk he threw." He glanced over the lineup again. "Very interesting," he added thoughtfully.

Kim stared at him. "What do you mean by that, Dad?"

Mr. Rollins shrugged. "Just what I said. Very interesting."

"That Franklin is a girl, Dad," explained Kim. "Her name's Jo. *J-o*. We've got two girls on the team. The other girl is Cathy Andrews."

Mr. Rollins lowered the paper and frowned. "I haven't seen Andy Franklin or Don Andrews in five or six years," he said. "Do Jo and Cathy have any brothers?"

Kim thought about it a moment. "Not that I know of," he said.

His father, still frowning, glanced back at the paper. "That sure is something, all right," he said.

The phone rang. Seconds later Mrs. Rollins called from the kitchen. "Pat! It's for you!"

"Coming!" Mr. Rollins said. He folded the paper and placed it on the coffee table. Rising, he looked at Kim.

"What's the name of your coach? Stag?"

"Yes. Gorman E. Stag," answered Kim.

"Him," replied Mr. Rollins, heading for the kitchen, "I've never heard of."

Kim didn't play in the game against the Fire Fighters. He coached first base during the first three innings, then was relieved by Cathy.

For the first two innings the Steelheads outhit the Fire Fighters and led 4 - 0. But by the fifth inning the Fire Fighters had climbed out of their slump and tied the score. It wasn't till then that Kim saw a change in Coach Stag. The coach was standing by the side of the dugout, dabbing his perspiring face with a handkerchief. Even then the coach didn't remove his glasses.

But he looked more nervous now than Kim had ever seen him. Was it because the Fire Fighters were gaining on the Steelheads? Kim wondered. Was it because the season was drawing swiftly toward its conclusion, and the Steelheads had to keep winning in order to win the championship?

For the first time since the baseball season had started, Kim felt angry with the coach. *So what if we lost?* Kim told himself. The game was supposed to be for fun first of all, wasn't it? Coach Stag only seemed concerned about one thing. Winning. *He's unbelievable!*

And for that matter, why doesn't he take off those sunglasses? What's behind them that he doesn't seem to want anyone to see?

Russ, on the mound for the Steelheads, kept the Fire Fighters from scoring again. Then he corked a double with one on in the sixth to win the game for the Steelheads, 5 - 4.

Kim couldn't help but notice the relief that came over the coach.

"Nice game, gang!" the coach said proudly. "That's another hill we've conquered! Just three more to go!"

Kim watched him turn to help Don Morgan pile the bats and balls into the equipment bag. He caught Eric's eye and motioned to him.

"Yeah?" said Eric as he came forward.

"Want to come with me to see where the coach lives?" he asked quietly.

Eric looked at him. "You still have that crazy idea that maybe he's a criminal?"

"I don't know. But there is *something* different about him, that's for sure."

Eric hesitated, then finally nodded. "Okay. I'll go with you."

10

SIX-SEVENTEEN BEAVER STREET
was at the opposite side of Blue Hills from
where Kim lived. He and Eric took a bus
there, arriving on the corner of Beaver and
Ford streets shortly before eight o'clock.

As they started walking down the six
hundred block of Beaver, Eric said, "Suppose we meet the coach and he wants to
know what we're doing here? What're we
going to tell him?"

Kim shrugged. "We'll be honest with
him."

Eric stared. "*Honest* with him?"

Kim looked directly at his perplexed friend. "We'll — okay, *I'll* ask him *why* he's so anxious to win the championship, and *why* he's picked *us* to play on his team. Look, he must be some kind of nut. Can you think of one single reason why he picked up a team composed of kids whose fathers all played on the same baseball team over twenty years ago? Can you?"

Eric shook his head. "No, I can't," he admitted. "Okay, come on. Let's get this over with before I change my mind."

They continued on their way, and presently stopped in front of 617, a tall, three-story, gray stone building with green, peeling shutters. A sign that seemed to be as old as the building read ROCKVILLE APTS.

"It's an apartment house," observed Kim.

"Looks like an old castle," said Eric.

Kim headed for the steps and the double

doors. Eric waited till he reached the steps, then followed him.

Gently Kim turned the knob, pushed the door in, and stepped inside, Eric at his heels. They found themselves inside a foyer leading to a long hallway and a staircase. On the wall near the staircase was a directory with mail slots. Kim read the names, finding only one that he recognized: *Bernard Reese — Apt. 12*.

"Eric!" he whispered. "Coach Stag's name isn't here!"

The boys looked at each other silently. "Well, what do we do now?" Eric asked finally.

"Let's see if Mr. Reese is in," Kim suggested. "He should be able to tell us something about Coach Stag, if he will."

Apartment 12 was on the second floor. Kim knocked on the door. No one answered. He knocked again, harder. Still no answer.

Disappointed, the boys started back

down the stairs, and saw a woman in a white print dress peering up at them.

"You boys looking for someone?" she asked.

"Mr. Reese," replied Kim. "I guess he's not in, though."

She smiled pleasantly. "Professor Reese, you mean. I think he's at the theater, directing a new play. Do you want to give me your names so that I can tell him you called on him? I'm Mrs. Pierce, the landlady."

The boys stopped halfway down the stairs, staring at her.

"*Professor* Reese?" Kim echoed.

"Yes."

Kim hesitated. "Well, we were really looking for Mr. Gorman Stag, our baseball coach, Mrs. Pierce," he confessed. "Professor Reese told us that he lived here."

The landlady paused and frowned. "Gorman Stag? I don't know of any Gorman —" She paused. Suddenly her eyes bright-

ened. "Wait a minute! Of course! He used to live here, but he moved! I really don't know where he moved to; he didn't tell me. A little man with thick glasses, right?"

Kim looked at her. "We've only seen him with dark sunglasses," he said.

"Oh, come to think of it, he did wear those sunglasses more than the plain ones," she said. "Well, look, I must be going. I was in the middle of doing my dishes when I heard you knocking on the door upstairs. Will you excuse me?"

"Of course," said Kim. "Thanks, ma'am."

She headed down the hall, and the boys headed out of the door.

"So Mr. Reese is really a professor," mused Kim, as he and Eric hurried down the steps to the sidewalk.

"And he's directing a new play," added Eric. "Know what? This whole thing is getting more mysterious every day."

They reached the bus stop on the corner and waited for their bus.

Kim said, "Did you notice the change on Mrs. Pierce's face when I told her that we were really looking for Coach Stag? I think she lied to us. I don't think that Coach Stag has ever lived in that apartment house."

Eric gazed confusedly at him. "Why would she lie to us? She's the landlady."

"I don't know," said Kim. "Maybe she and Professor Reese have cooked up something about Coach Stag."

"Why? Look, if you still think that Coach Stag is a crook — which I think is crazy — why would Professor Reese protect him?" exclaimed Eric doubtfully. "Have you thought about that?"

Kim, looked at him, his face rigid. "Maybe Mrs. Pierce is the only other person who knows, and they're all involved in something together," he answered. "Eric, this sounds crazy, but I've made up my mind. The next time I see Professor Reese I'm going to ask him just who, or what, Coach Stag is. I don't see any reason why we shouldn't know who he is, and why he's so darned anxious to win the championship with a team whose kids are sons and daughters of fathers who played on the same team twenty years ago!"

It wasn't until the game against the Blue Jays that Kim saw Professor Reese again. He shored up enough courage to ask the professor about the coach, but couldn't find the opportunity. There was always someone too close by. And Kim felt that the question he wanted to ask the professor was of such a nature that he had to be sure no one else heard it.

The game was another close one. Going into the fifth inning, the Blue Jays were ahead, 8 - 7, and again Kim saw how the coach was reacting. Coach Stag was visibly worried, pacing in the small area at the side of the dugout like a caged animal.

Nick Forson's double in left center field, followed by an error by the Blue Jays' left fielder, evened up the score. Kim noticed that the coach had stopped his pacing now, and that a look of renewed hope had returned to his face.

Eric pounded the hit that brought in the tie-breaking run. The sixth inning went scoreless, and the game went to the Steelheads, 9 - 8.

"Nice game, gang," praised the coach, wiping the sweat beads off his lips with a handkerchief. "Winning is the key. Only two more games to go. All we've got to do is win one of them, and the championship is ours. Isn't that great, huh? Isn't that just great?"

Kim looked at him, and again felt that the coach was pressing the team too hard.

Why is it so important to you to win the

championship, Coach? Kim wanted to ask him. *Who are you really, anyway?*

But he reasoned that he'd have to wait until the next game — or the game after that — to really find out.

11

A WEEK LATER THE STEELHEADS played the Blue Jays again. After having beaten them twice, the Steelheads went onto the field with the confidence that they could repeat their win.

Kim watched the game from the bench, and after a while couldn't believe his eyes as he saw the Blue Jays come up with the greatest game he had ever seen them play.

Two homers and three triples were included in the rampage, yet Coach Stag let Russ Coletti pitch the entire game. And, as inning after inning went by, and the Blue Jays piled up one run after another to the Steelheads' scattered few, Kim saw the coach sitting at the end of the bench, his arms crossed over his chest, his face like a plastic statue's.

Coach Stag had yelled a lot to his charges during the early innings, but when he seemed to realize that his yelling was doing no good he stopped and let the game take its course. It was as if he knew that every bit of his coaching knowledge wasn't enough to stop the powerful — or was it lucky? — Blue Jays.

Kim saw that the professor, Bernie Reese, was sitting quietly next to the coach. *I wish he were alone,* Kim thought. *I'd ask him about Coach Stag. I'm not afraid to anymore.*

In the sixth inning the Blue Jays were leading, 13 - 4. There were two outs and Russ was up.

"Strike!" barked the ump as the Blue Jays pitcher slipped one by him.

Kim saw Coach Stag get up and leave the dugout. He saw Don gazing at the coach, the gaze lingering for a while before he glanced back at the batter. His face looked as sad as the coach's.

Kim saw his opportunity now to speak to Professor Reese alone, and quickly went over to him.

"Professor Reese," he said softly.

"Hi, Kim," said the professor. "I was wondering when you'd start calling me that. Mrs. Pierce told me that you and Eric came to see me a few days ago."

Kim nodded. "Yes. It's about Coach Stag." He paused, his heart pounding. "We've been wondering about him, sir."

"I expected you would eventually," said the professor calmly. "Especially you, since you're the only member on the team who had played so little baseball before."

Kim looked at him. His nerves tightened

98

up. He glanced briefly at the plate as a second strike was called on Russ.

"Well, those dark sunglasses that he always wears, and his kind of mysterious ways, make some of the kids think he's a crook," said Kim, feeling foolish the moment he said it.

Professor Reese laughed. "No, he's not a crook, Kim! He's a really fine human being! Surprisingly, he has his own reason for doing what he's been doing during this baseball season. When he told me of his idea I wanted to talk him out of it. I thought it was kind of silly, until he gave me his reason why he wanted to do it."

Kim's eyes widened, and he stared at the professor.

Just then he heard a *crack!* and glanced around to see Russ's fly ball sailing out to center field. But even before he saw the fielder catch it, ending the ball game, Kim heard Professor Reese saying, "Well, he was never allowed to play when he was a kid because of his poor eyesight. That's why he wanted to coach a team this year, to prove to certain people that in spite of his not ever playing baseball, he could put a special team together and win the championship."

"Did it have something to do with our fathers' team of twenty years ago?" Kim asked.

"It did, but that's all I'll tell you now, Kim. Anyway," the professor rose, "the game's over. There's only one more to go. We've got to win it, or all of Coach Stag's hard work and ambition will be wasted, and he'll be heartbroken. So don't you see, Kim? You and the rest of the team must do your best next week against the Red Arrows. You'll learn the whole story about Coach Stag then."

All the professor's words did was increase Kim's anxiety. Bubbling with excitement, Kim couldn't wait to get home to have another talk with his father.

In less than two minutes he found out what he wanted to know. His heart pounding like a hammer, he gathered up a pencil and paper and began to figure out Coach Stag's true identity.

Finally the day of the Red Arrows - Steelheads game arrived. Knowing now why Coach Stag wanted so desperately to win the championship, Kim was glad that he was playing. And he'd play his heart out, too, he promised himself.

The Red Arrows had first bats.

"Get 'em outa there, Doug!" Kim yelled in right field.

"Breeze it by him, ol' boy!" cried A. J.

Right off, the Arrows' Mick Davis connected with a single, then advanced to second as Hank Stone drove a blistering grounder through third-baseman Eric Marsh's legs. After that Doug seemed to try pitching more cautiously, throwing to the outside corner to Jim Kramer. The pitches were balls, and Jim didn't bite. Then Doug laid one directly over the heart of the plate, and — *Crack!* Jim smashed it to right center for a double, scoring two runs.

"Bear down in there, Doug!" yelled Kim as catcher Ken Dooley stepped into the batter's box.

Ken, the Red Arrows' long-distance hitter, looked menacing as he waved his bat over his shoulder, his eyes centered on Doug.

Doug blazed a strike by him. Ken swung at the next and missed it for strike two. Then he blasted a high fly to center field, which Cathy got under and caught easily.

Fred Tuttle, up next, singled to continue the Red Arrows' relentless drive, scoring Jim. Joe Fedderson belted a streaking grounder to short that Brad fumbled, leaving Joe safe at first and Fred on second. Then Duke lambasted a long drive to right center field that he tried to stretch into a triple. But Eric, catching Jo Franklin's throw after she had caught Kim's peg from deep right, tagged out Duke as the Red Arrow runner tried to slide past him. Two outs.

Eddie Noles continued the batting spree with a sharp single over second. But that was it as Jack Moon, the Red Arrows' left-handed pitcher, went down swinging.

"Five to nothing!" Larry exclaimed as he and Kim came trotting in to the dugout. "Man! That's some start!"

"You should've taken me out, Coach," said Doug dismally as he flung his glove against the dugout wall. "Everything I threw they hit."

"Okay. Now it's our turn," said the coach. "And remember, it's our last game. It's the big one. Win this, and we'll have a party that's a *party!*"

Kim smiled at him. *Coach*, he wanted to

103

say, *I don't know how you got away with it all this time. But you certainly did. And I'm sorry I doubted your motives before. After finding out what they are, I'm with you all the way!*

12

IT WAS ONE, TWO, THREE for the Steelheads as Eric struck out, Larry flied out, and Nick grounded out.

"Hey, you guys!" yelled Kim as he ran out on the field with his teammates. "We can't let Coach Stag down like this! We've got to start hitting that ball!"

"Look who's talking," Brad snorted. "When are *you* going to start hitting? Next year? It's too late this year."

"Well, I'm doing my best," Kim replied.

"For never having played on a team

before, I think that Kim's done very well," said Cathy.

Thanks, Cathy, Kim wanted to say, and wondered how many others felt as she did.

"This is our last game, and we still don't know why Coach Stag picked us to play on his team, and why he's been so anxious to win the championship," said Larry.

"Well, *I* know," said Kim, grinning.

"You do?" Larry's eyebrows shot skyward. The others stared at Kim. "Well — why?"

Suddenly Kim wished he hadn't opened his big mouth. But it was too late now. "We'll all find out at the end of this game," he said. "Let's just play our best game ever, that's all."

"Why are you keeping it a secret, if you know?" asked A. J. curiously. "What's so important about it?"

"I said that we'll all find out. Come on," he added, breaking for his right-field position. "Let's win this ol' ball game for Coach Stag!"

"Right!" cried Cathy.

The top of the Red Arrows' batting order was up. As Mick Davis walked, Kim feared that another fat inning was in the offing. But Hank hit into a double play, and Jim flied out.

"Nice going, gang," said the coach, appearing less tense now than he did after that first grueling half inning.

A. J., leading off in the bottom half of the second inning, earned a walk. Cathy bunted him down to second, sacrificing herself on a quick throw to first by third baseman Hank Stone. Kim, hoping to score A. J., grounded out to short, and Brad popped out to the catcher. Three outs.

Ken Dooley led off for the Red Arrows in the top of the third. Doug managed to squeak two strikes by him, then Ken took a toehold on the third pitch and drove it to left center for a double.

Again Kim expected the hit to be the beginning of something big for the Red Arrows, but relief swept over him as Fred Tuttle flied out to left, and both Joe Fedderson and Duke Pierce struck out.

"Nice pitching, Doug!" Kim praised the right-hander as he came running in.

"He's going to be another Catfish Hunter!" Nick Forson smiled.

Jo, leading off for the Steelheads, waited out Jack Moon's pitches, then flied out to right. Doug, drawing loud applause from the crowd as he stepped to the batter's box, corked Jack's first pitch for a double. Eric drove him in on a single through short, then got out as Larry hit into a double play — 5 - 1, Red Arrows' favor.

"Come on, gang!" cried the coach. "Just hold 'em!"

The Steelheads did, permitting only one batter, Jack Moon, to reach first base.

Nick Forson led off in the bottom of the fourth with a sharp single through the pitcher's box. A. J., waiting out Jack's pitches, finally clouted one to deep left for a triple, scoring Nick. The Steelheads' bench sprang to life as the scoring gap narrowed.

"Keep it going, Cathy!" Kim shouted.

Cathy pounded out a fly to right field. It was caught, but A. J. tagged up, then ran in to score. Kim, anxious to get on base, popped out to third. Brad drew a walk, then advanced to second on Jo's hit through short. Two on, two outs, and Doug was up. A long drive could tie the score.

Jack stretched, and pitched. *Crack!* It was a solid blow to left field! But not deep enough. Jim Kramer trotted back, leaped, and made a sparkling one-handed catch to end the threat — 5 - 3, Red Arrows.

Applause greeted Jim as he strode to the plate to start off the top of the fifth inning. Cracking no smile, he watched the first pitch come in, then belted the next for a clean single.

Ken Dooley, batting for the third time, took a called strike, then two balls, then leaned into a chest-high pitch with apparently all the power he could muster. The sound of bat meeting ball was like a rifle blast. The ball that rocketed out to deep left field was like a bullet. It went over the fence for a home run, boosting the Red Arrows' score to 7.

"Oh, no!" Kim moaned, almost hearing the bell of doom for the Steelheads. And for the coach. What chance was there now for the Steelheads to win the game? A 7 - 3 lead was almost too much to expect to overcome.

Poor coach. He'll never get over this if we lose, Kim told himself sadly.

Fred Tuttle, up next, flied out. Then Joe grounded out to short and Duke struck out on three pitches. Relieved, Kim sprinted off the field.

"Let's get those runs back!" he cried spiritedly. "Come on, guys! We're as good as they are!"

"We've got to be better," said Nick, removing his catcher's gear.

Eric said nothing as he picked up a bat and stepped to the plate. In five pitches he was granted a walk. Larry, up next, got hit by a pitch, dropped his bat, and trotted to first. Eric advanced to second.

Nick, the back of his shirt damp with sweat, belted a high, sky-reaching fly to center. Duke Pierce moved back four steps and caught it.

Then A. J. stepped to the plate, drawing loud applause from the crowd. He had walked and tripled his first two times up.

This time he managed only to pop up to

Two outs, and Cathy was up. She had bunted the first time at bat, and flied out the second time. What was she going to do now? The Steelheads' bench was silent as a morgue.

"Come on, gang!" cried the coach. "A little life! How about it?"

At once the bench came alive. "Get a hit, Cath!"

"Drive 'em in, Cath!"

Jack Moon stretched, pitched, and Cathy swung. *Crack!* The blow, a solid blast to left center field, went for a double! Eric scored. But Larry, guided by the third-base coach, clung to third.

Kim strode to the plate, his ears still ringing from the cheers the fans were giving Cathy.

"Okay, Kim!" they yelled to him. "Keep up the merry-go-round! Hit that apple!"

He did, a long, smashing blow to deep left field! He could tell by the sound and the feel of his bat striking the ball that it was the best hit he had connected with so far this year. Dropping his bat, he ran to first, then looked toward left field and saw the ball sailing out of sight over the fence.

The cheers that rose from the fans brought a lump to his throat that didn't leave until after he had crossed home plate.

Brad kept up the spree with a single, gaining second as Jo walked. But Doug's caught fly to right field ended the fat inning. Red Arrows 7, Steelheads 7.

"Nice hit, Kim," said the coach proudly. "We needed that badly."

Kim smiled. "Thanks, Coach," he said warmly.

Eddie Noles, leading off for the Red Arrows in the top of the sixth, flied out to center. Jack fouled two pitches, then grounded out to short. Mick, after looking over two over-the-inside-corner strikes, belted a long drive to right center that looked as if it might turn into an inside-the-park home run. But Kim's quick throw to Jo, and her snap to Nick, forced Mick back

113

to third after he tried to make a dash for home.

Nervousness began to spread among the Steelheads. All the Red Arrows needed now was a hit to break the tie and possibly win the ball game.

Crack! A long, sharp blow to center field! Cathy ran forward, reached for the ball by her shoelaces — and caught it! Three outs!

Kim let out a sigh of relief as a thunder of applause rose from the Steelheads' fans for Cathy.

Eric, leading off in the bottom of the sixth inning, flied out to right.

"Come on, Larry!" Kim cried. "Get on!"

Larry smashed a single through the pitcher's box, then advanced to second as Joe Fedderson missed Nick's grass-scorching grounder. One out, two runners on, and A. J. was up.

He took a called strike, then two balls, then laced a pitch to right center. Across the plate raced Larry, and the ball game was over!

The Steelheads won the game, 8 - 7, and the championship was theirs!

An hour later the Steelheads, including Coach Stag and Professor Reese, were at the city park, celebrating their victory.

A huge white cake sat on the middle of a picnic table. On it was a statue of a baseball coach, and in his hands was a rolled-up scroll. A bakery had made the cake and the statue.

Kim's pulse tingled as he saw the coach look at the cake.

"Hey, what a surprise!" exclaimed the coach. "Whose idea was it?"

"Kim's," said Cathy.

The coach glanced at Kim. "I had a hunch," he said.

Kim grinned. "We all wondered why you picked up a team from all over the city, including me, who never played on a team before," he confessed. "And we wondered very much why you worked so hard to make us a championship team, so Eric and I did some detective work. We found out that the fathers of all us kids had played on the same team over twenty years ago."

"Well!" said the coach. "Smart deduction! Go on."

"We also found out that each of us played the same positions as our fathers had, too. And the reason you asked Cathy and Jo to play with us was because there weren't any boys in their families."

"Clever." The coach's smile broadened.

"But we still couldn't figure out who *you* were, or why you wanted to win the championship so badly," Kim went on, "until Professor Reese gave me a hint."

"Oh? What was that?" asked the coach.

The team stood still as statues, listening attentively to Kim's every word.

"He said that you were never given a chance to play baseball when you were a kid because of your poor eyesight," explained Kim. "When I asked my dad if he knew of a kid like that, he told me. Gates Morgan!"

"But my name is Stag," said the coach. "Gorman E. Stag."

Kim laughed. "An anagram of your real name — Gates Morgan!"

"Gates Morgan?" Doug echoed. "You mean he's Don's father?"

"Right!" said Kim.

"I can't believe it!" Brad cried.

Simultaneously, cries of disbelief sprang from the other Steelheads' players as the coach removed his sunglasses, lifted off a red wig, then slowly removed a film of makeup from his face, and dabs of cotton out of his mouth.

"Mr. Morgan!" exclaimed A. J. dumbfoundedly. "It is you! Why in the world did you disguise yourself?"

Gates Morgan smiled cheerfully. "Well, I —" He shrugged. "It's hard to explain."

"I'll do it for him," intervened Professor Reese. "Gates Morgan is basically an actor. He's in the new play I'm directing, and it was his being in it that gave him the idea to play his role of Gorman E. Stag in a real-life drama. It also gave him a chance to prove to himself, and to your fathers who had played on the team on which he was only allowed to be an equipment handler, that he was very capable of coaching a team to a championship. Disguising himself was just a pleasurable opportunity for him to see if he was able to fool his audience. He almost succeeded too, except for a few of you who got very nosy." He chuckled, adding, "I told Gates that some of you even went as far as to think that he was a criminal!"

Gates Morgan, and the Steelheads team, broke out in laughter.

"Hardly that," mused the actor-coach.

"I'd like to add one more thing to what Bernie said, though. I coached, but you all played like champs — and you never thought you could." Then he turned to Kim. "By the way, Kim, there's a role open for a young tennis player in the next play that Bernie will direct. I'd like you to consider playing the part."

Kim's eyebrows shot skyward. "But I've never played tennis, Mr. Morgan!" he said.

Gates Morgan smiled. "So? You had never played baseball before, either, had you?"